You'll Never Guess!

You'll Never Guess!

Fiona Dunbar

Dial Books for Young Readers New York

For my mother

First published in the United States 1991 by
Dial Books for Young Readers · A Division of Penguin Books USA Inc.
375 Hudson Street · New York, New York 10014

Published in Great Britain by Hutchinson Children's Books
An imprint of Century Hutchinson Ltd.
Copyright © 1990 by Fiona Dunbar

Library of Congress Cataloging in Publication Data
Dunbar, Fiona. You'll never guess!
Summary: Two children look at shadows of images that seem
familiar and try to guess what each is, with unexpected results.
1. Literary recreations—Juvenile literature.
2. Picture puzzles—Juvenile literature.
[1. Picture puzzles] I. Title.
GV1493.D89 1991 793.73 90-2795
ISBN 0-8037-0871-8

You'll never guess what this is!

Could it be my friend Lisa?

No, silly! It's the dog from next door.

This is easy — it's a palm tree.

Wrong! It's a movie star in a crazy hat.

Quick, hide! It's a huge ferocious lion!

Relax. . . . It's just Rover,
bringing in a sheep.

I know this one — it's a pepper grinder.

Sorry! It's a doll from Japan, dressed in a kimono.

Now, this *must* be a teapot.

No! It's a little boy riding an elephant.

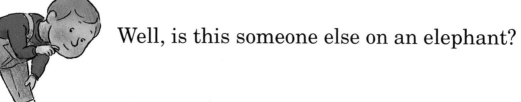

Well, is this someone else on an elephant?

Surprise! It's a snake, just finished with lunch.

I'm sure this is a snail. What else could it be?

Look! It's Grandma, knitting a muffler.

If this isn't a cat, I'll eat my hat.

I hope you're hungry, because it's a sly old fox instead.

Here's a car. It's *definitely* a car.

You're sure?

Absolutely positive.

Ha! Fooled you.

It's a turtle on roller skates.

Okay, *you* guess this one, if you're so smart.

That's obvious. . . . It's a hen laying an egg.

See, it's not that easy. It's Dad, having his breakfast.

All right, I'll give you a clue for this one:
It used to be a prince.

That's simple — it's a king.

Wrong again! It's a frog, waiting to be kissed.

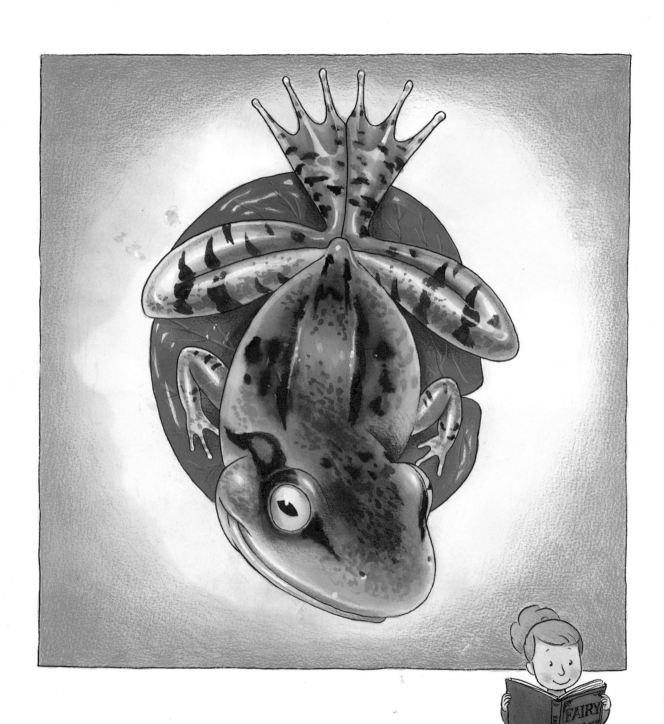

(I think he'll have to wait a long time, too.)

Look out! It's a monster with lots of arms and legs and heads!

It's okay, calm down. It's only the movie star and the dogs and the sheep and the doll from Japan and the little boy on the elephant and the snake and Grandma and the sly old fox and the turtle and Dad and the frog!

Wow! So this is just another bunch of people and animals.... *Isn't it?*

OH NO, IT ISN'T!

QUICK . . .

RUN!

Where do you think we'll hide?

You'll never guess!